This book belongs to:

· · · · · · · · · · · · · · · ·

For my Mama,
with all my wild heart.

 E.H.

This is a fifth edition published in 2015 by Flying Eye Books,
an imprint of Nobrow Ltd. 62 Great Eastern Street, London, EC2A 3QR

Published in the US by Nobrow (US) inc

Printed in Belgium by Proost Industries nv on FSC assured paper

ISBN 978-1-909263-08-6

Order from www.flyingeyebooks.com

Wild

by Emily Hughes

FLYING EYE BOOKS

LONDON · NEW YORK

No one remembered how she came to the woods,
but all knew it was right.

The whole forest took her as their own.

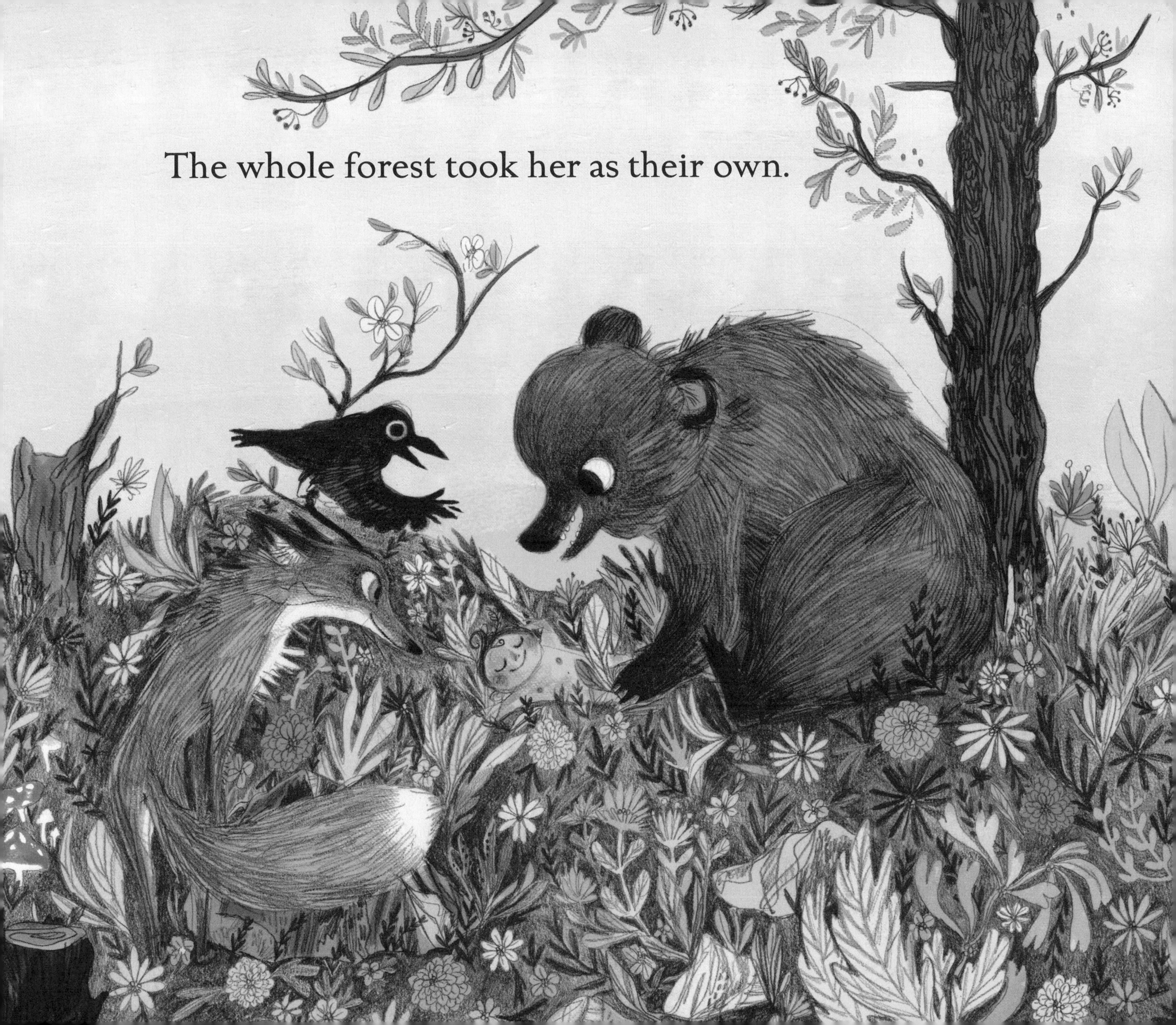

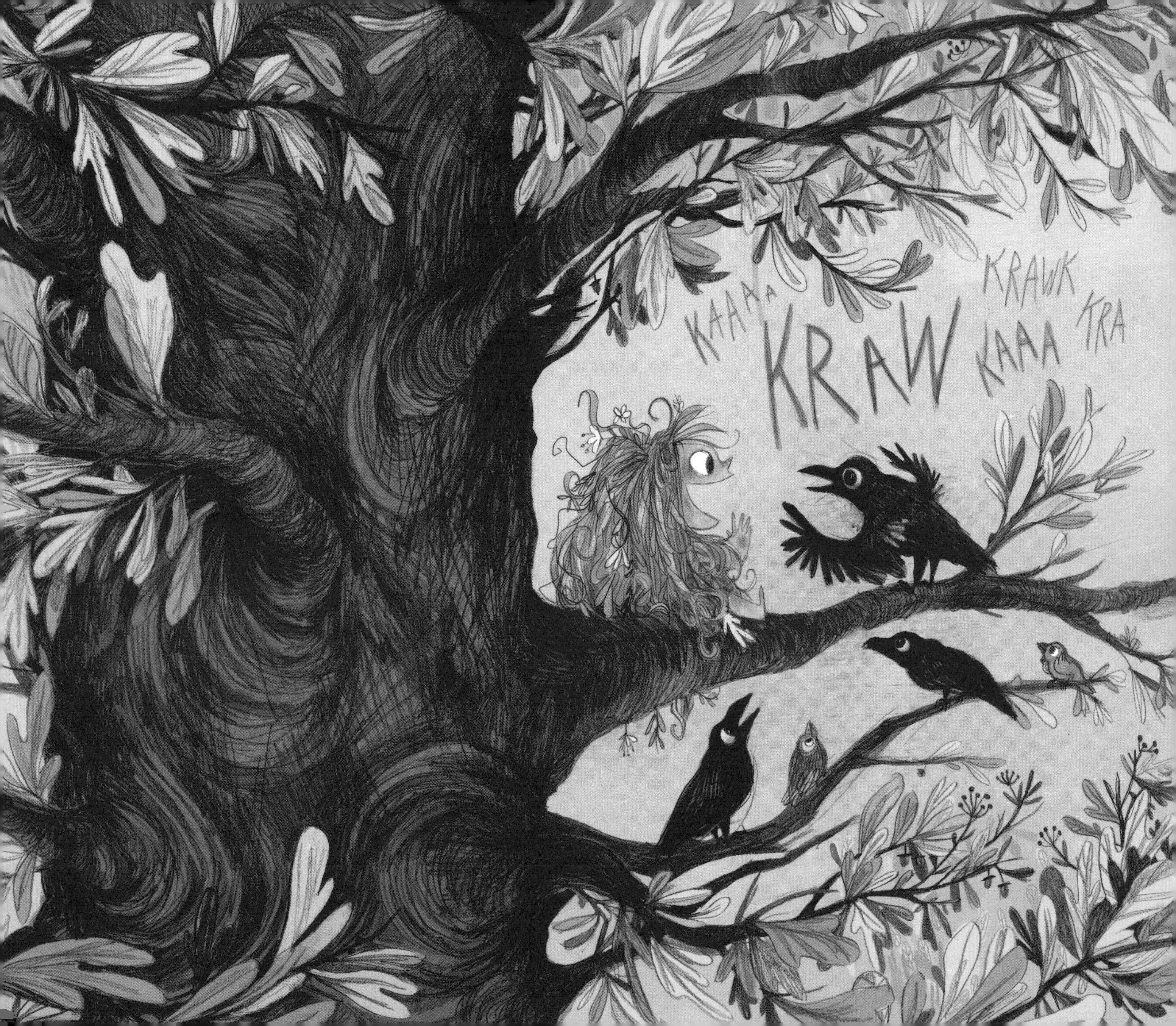
KAAAA
KRAW
KRAWK
KAAA
KRA

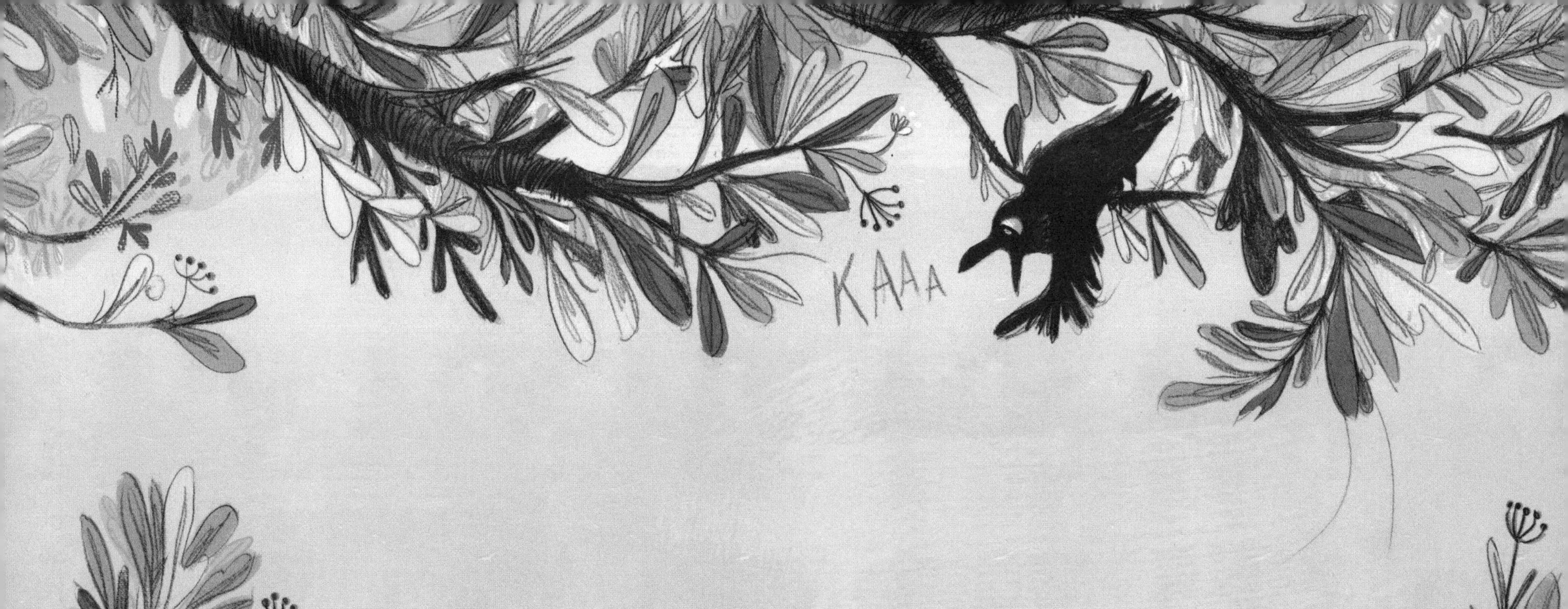
KAAA

Bird taught her how to speak.

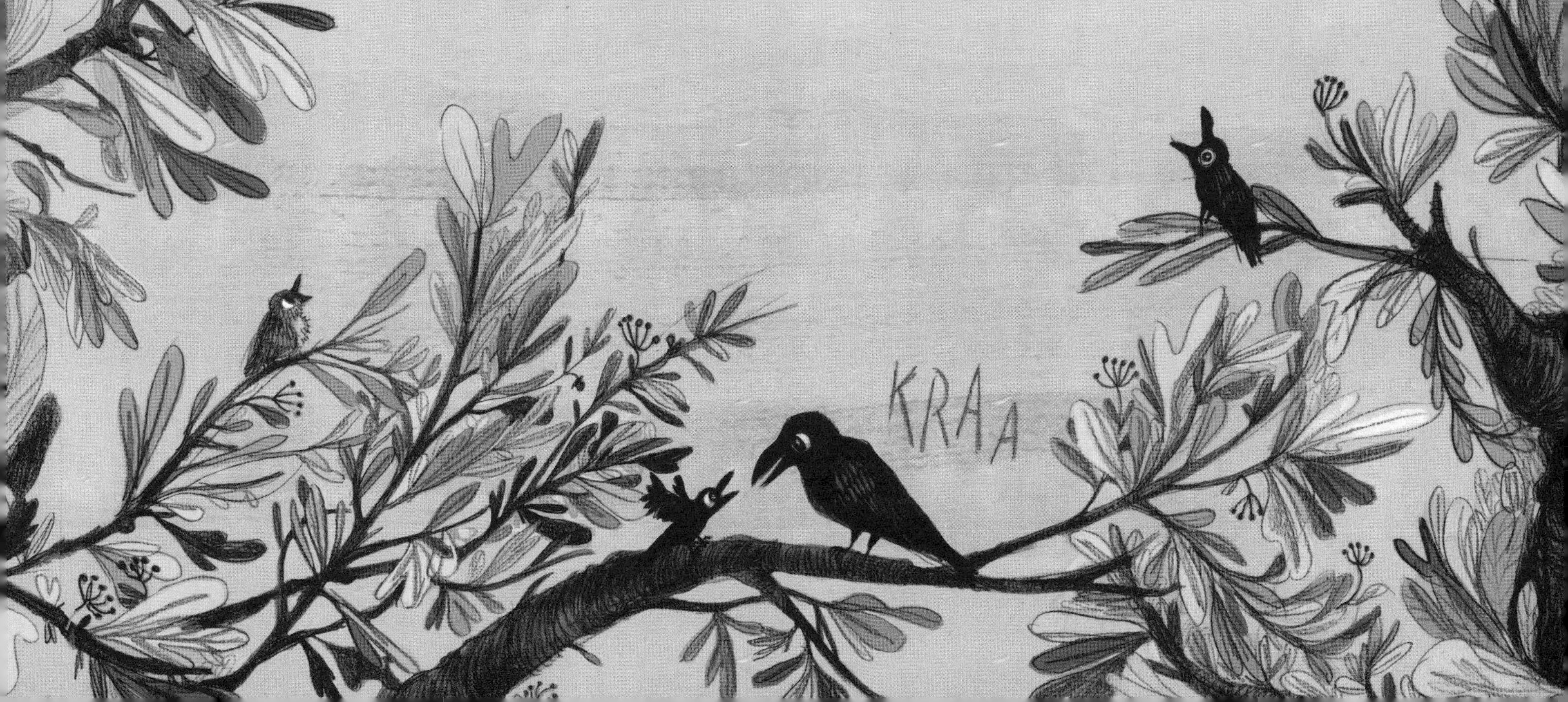
KRAA

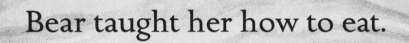

Bear taught her how to eat.

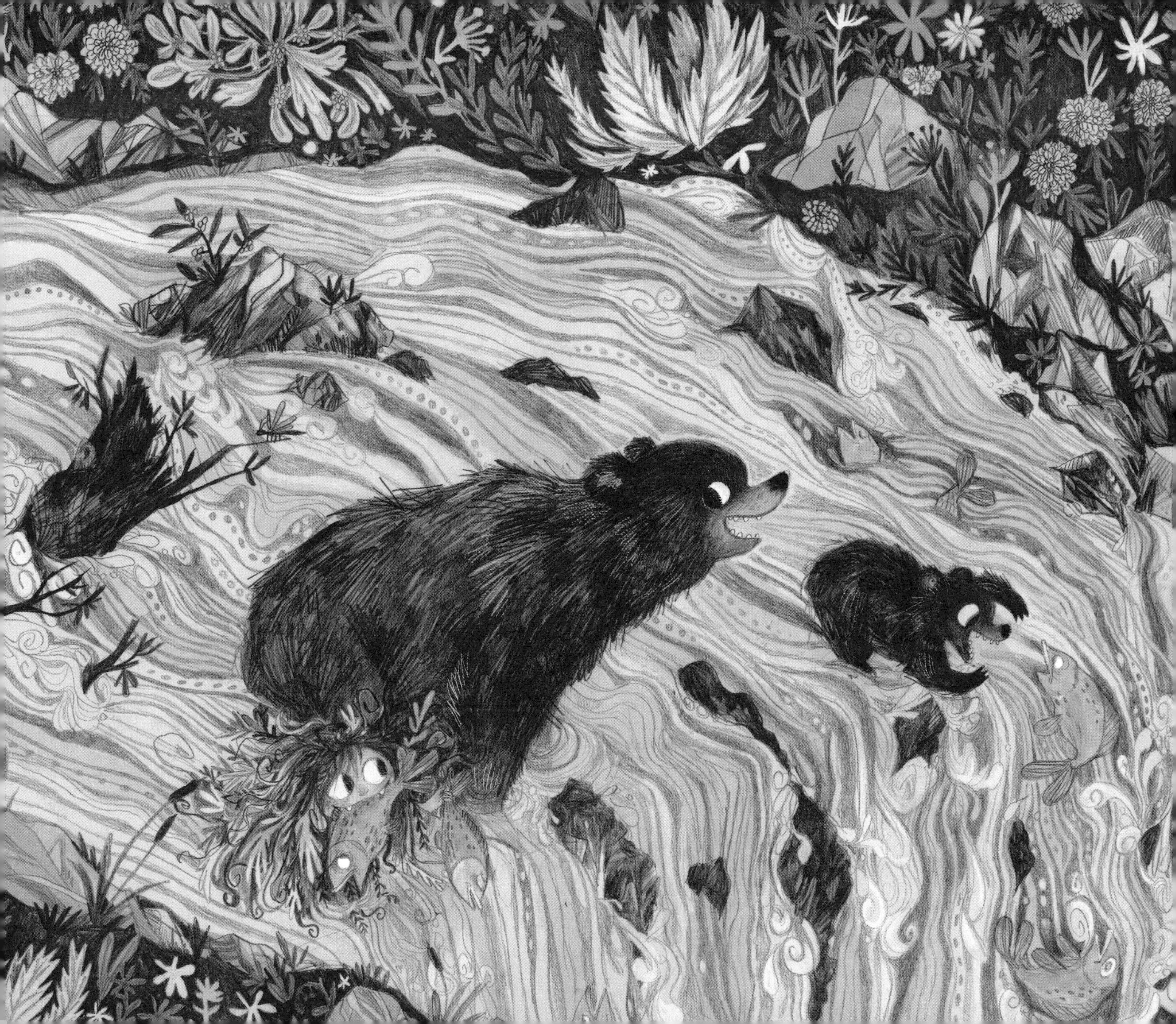

Fox taught her how to play.

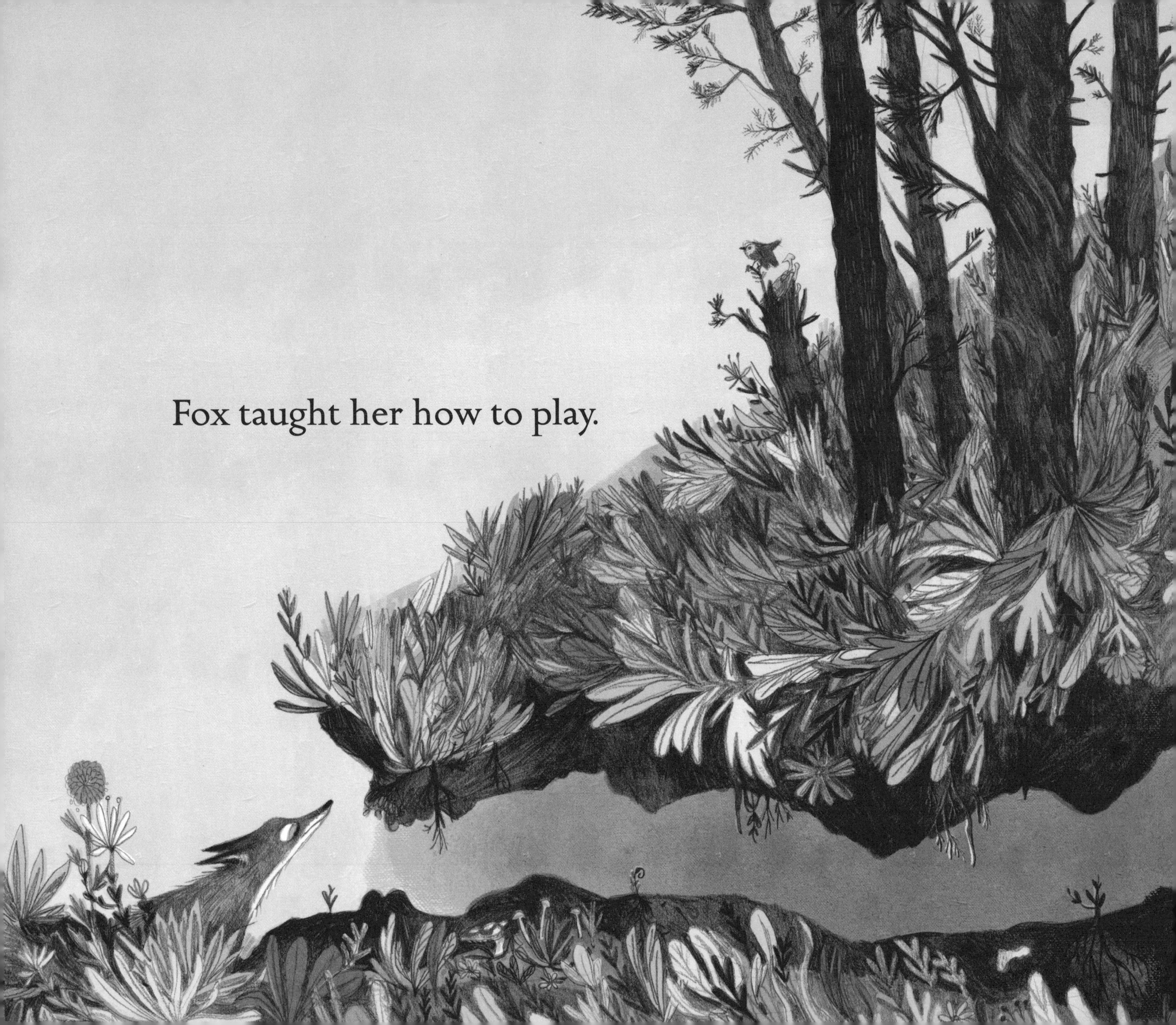

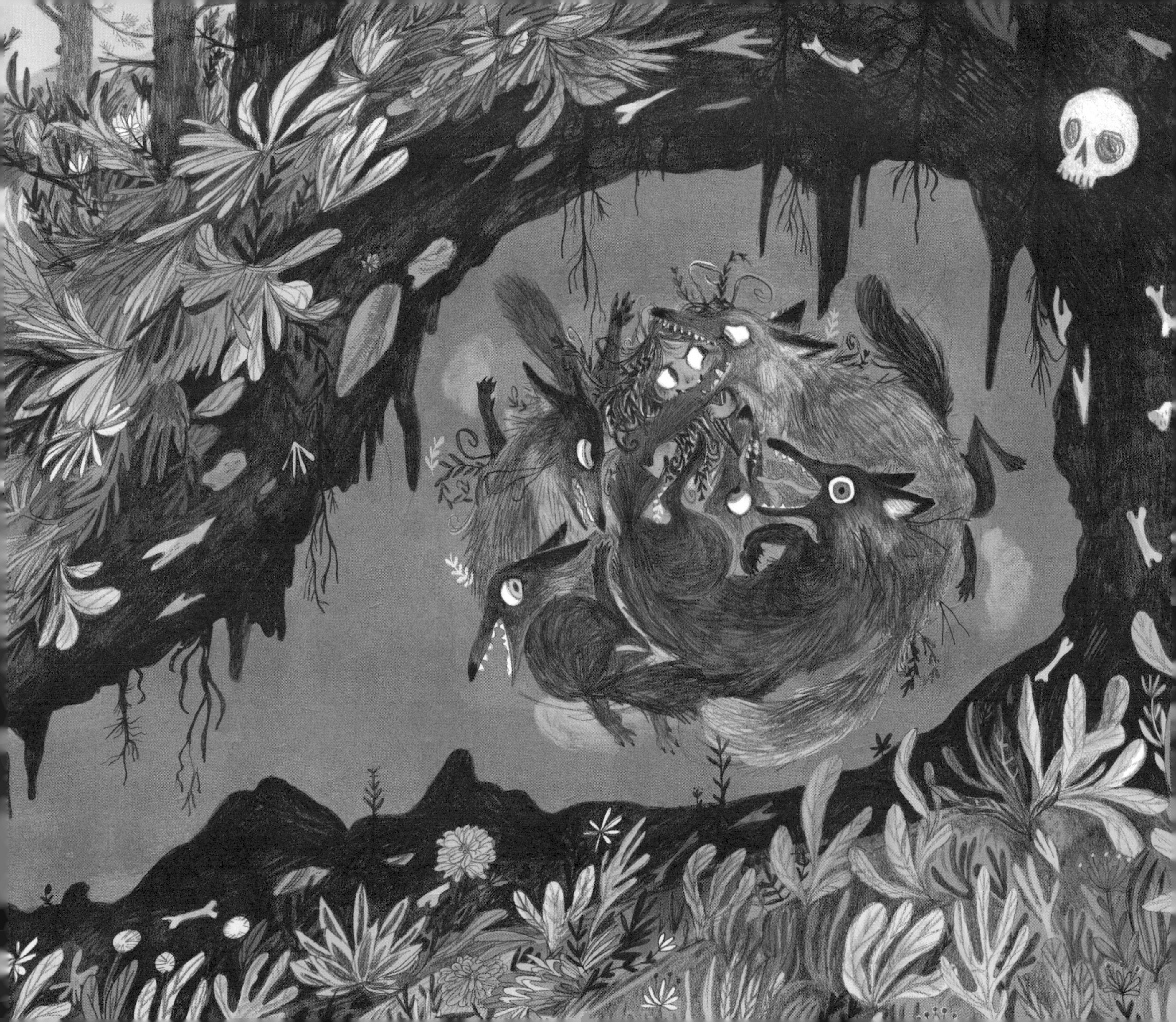

And she understood, and was happy.

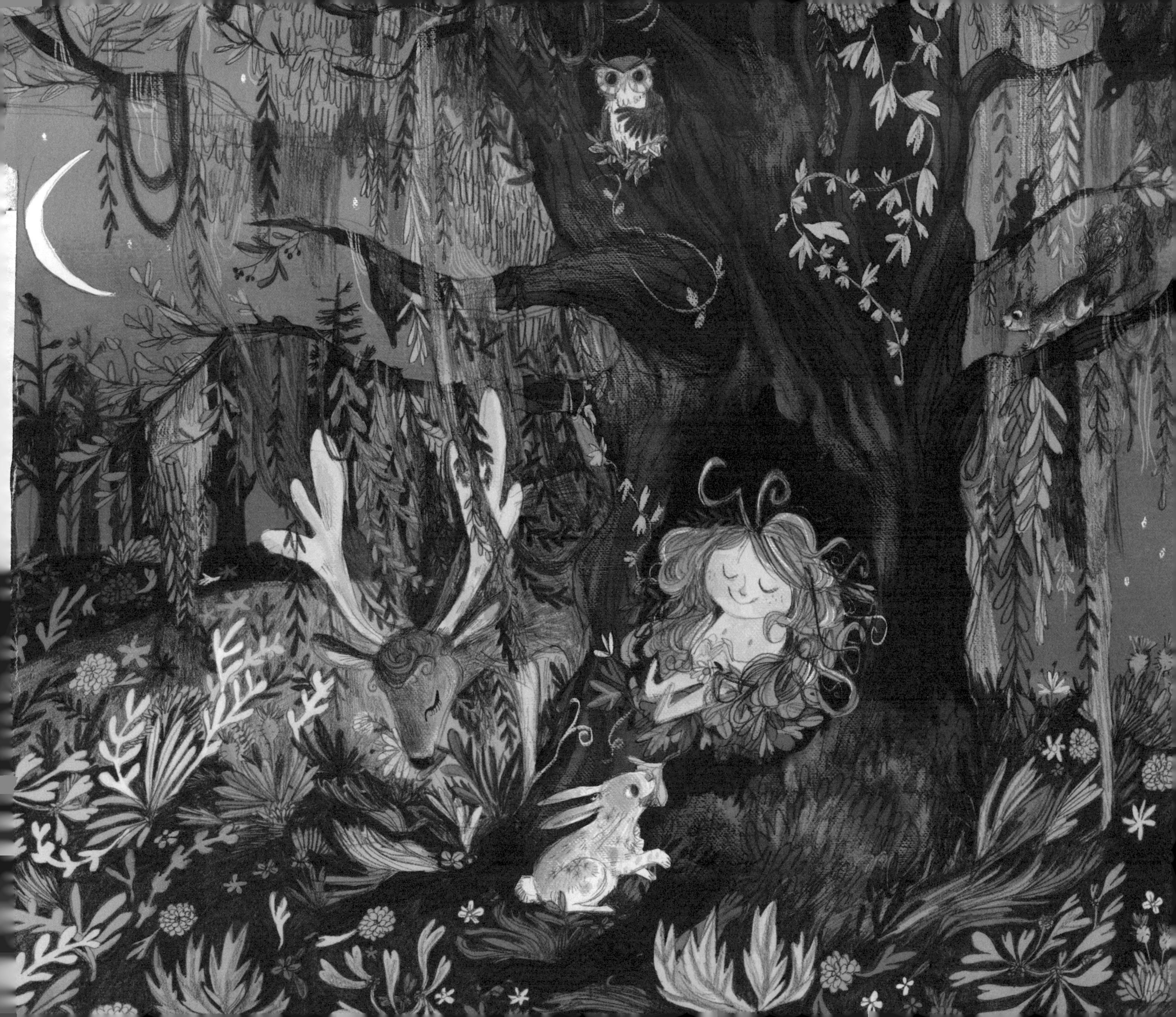

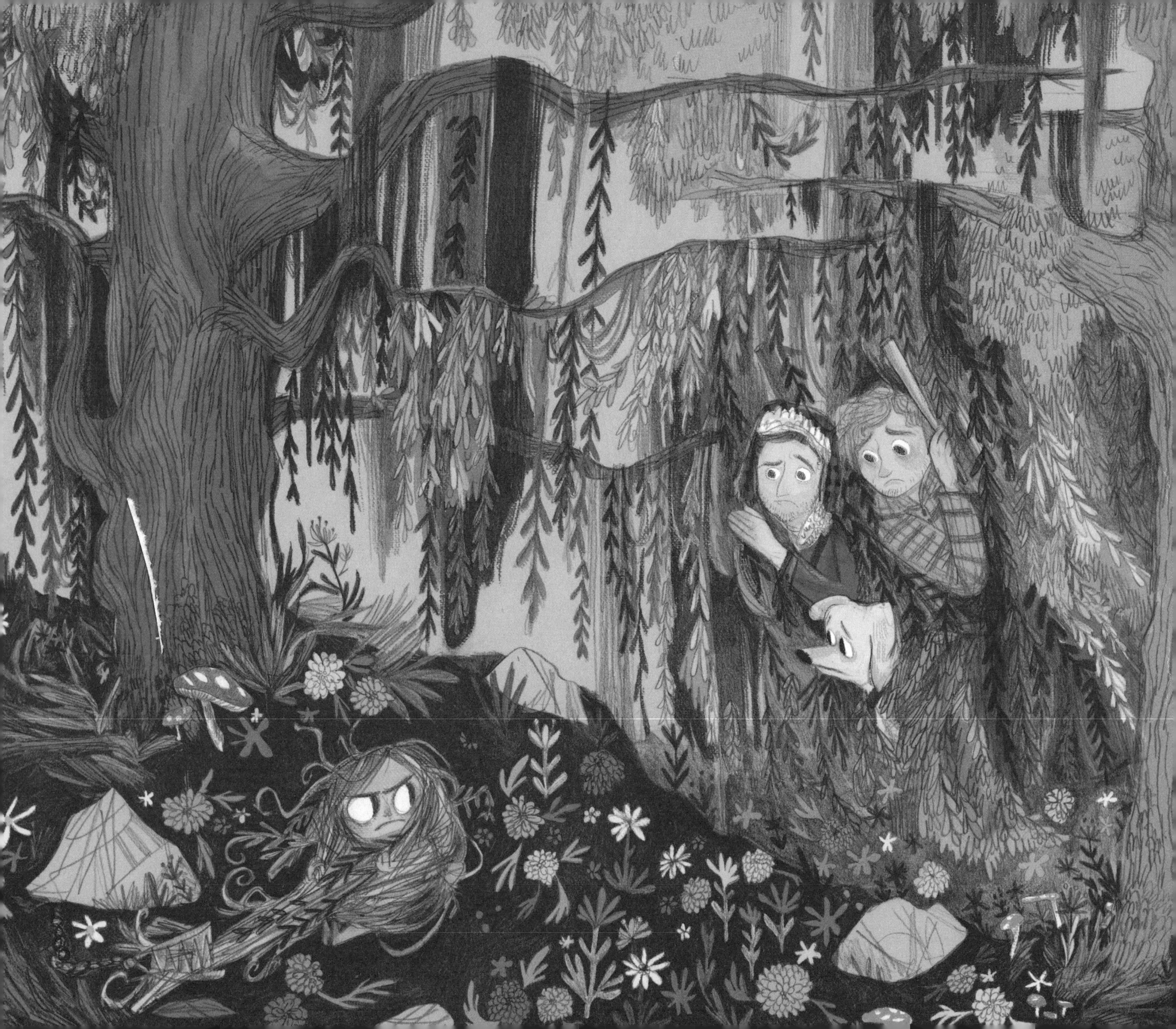

One day she met some new animals in the forest...

They found her strange...

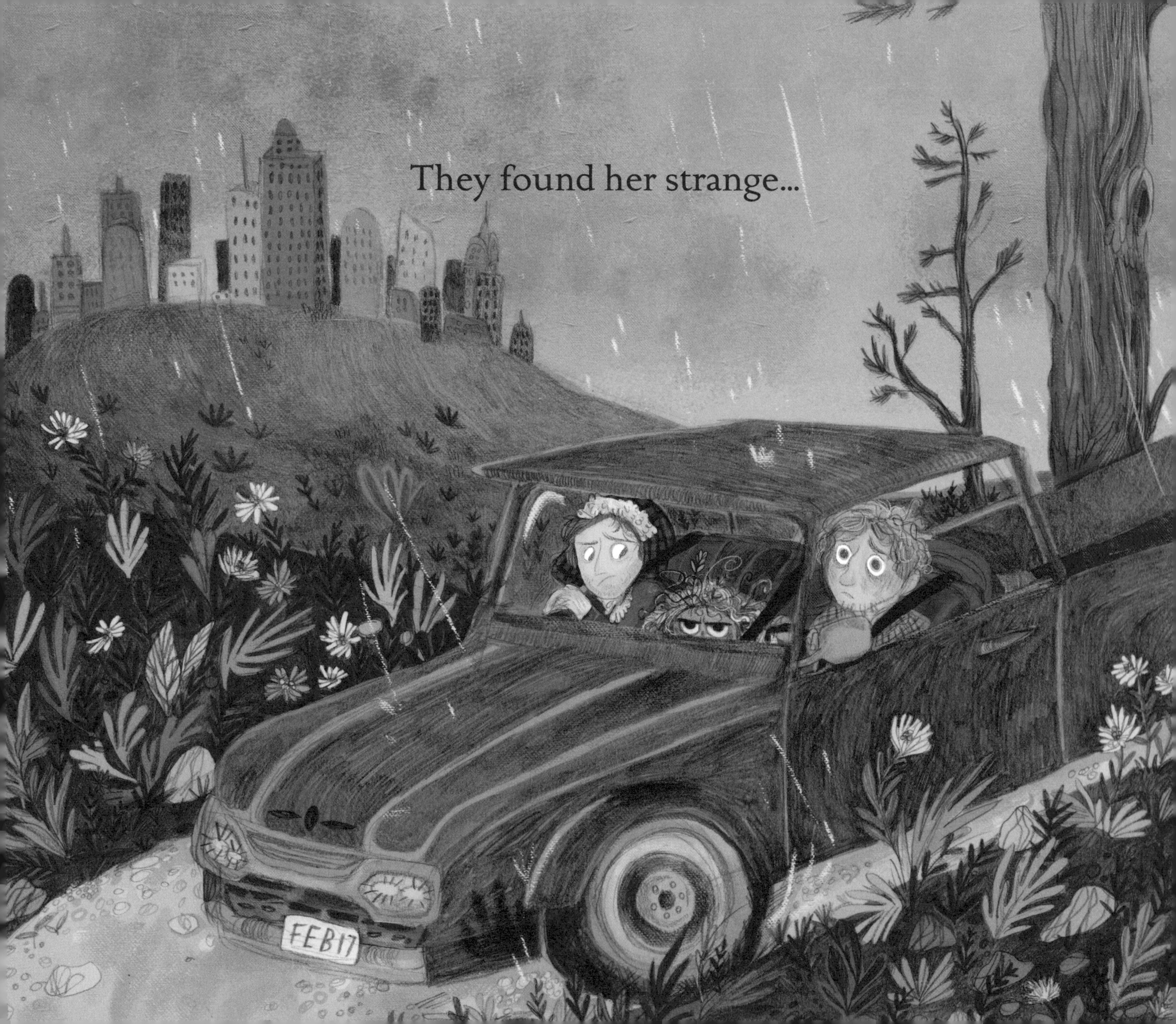
FEB17

...and she found them strange too.

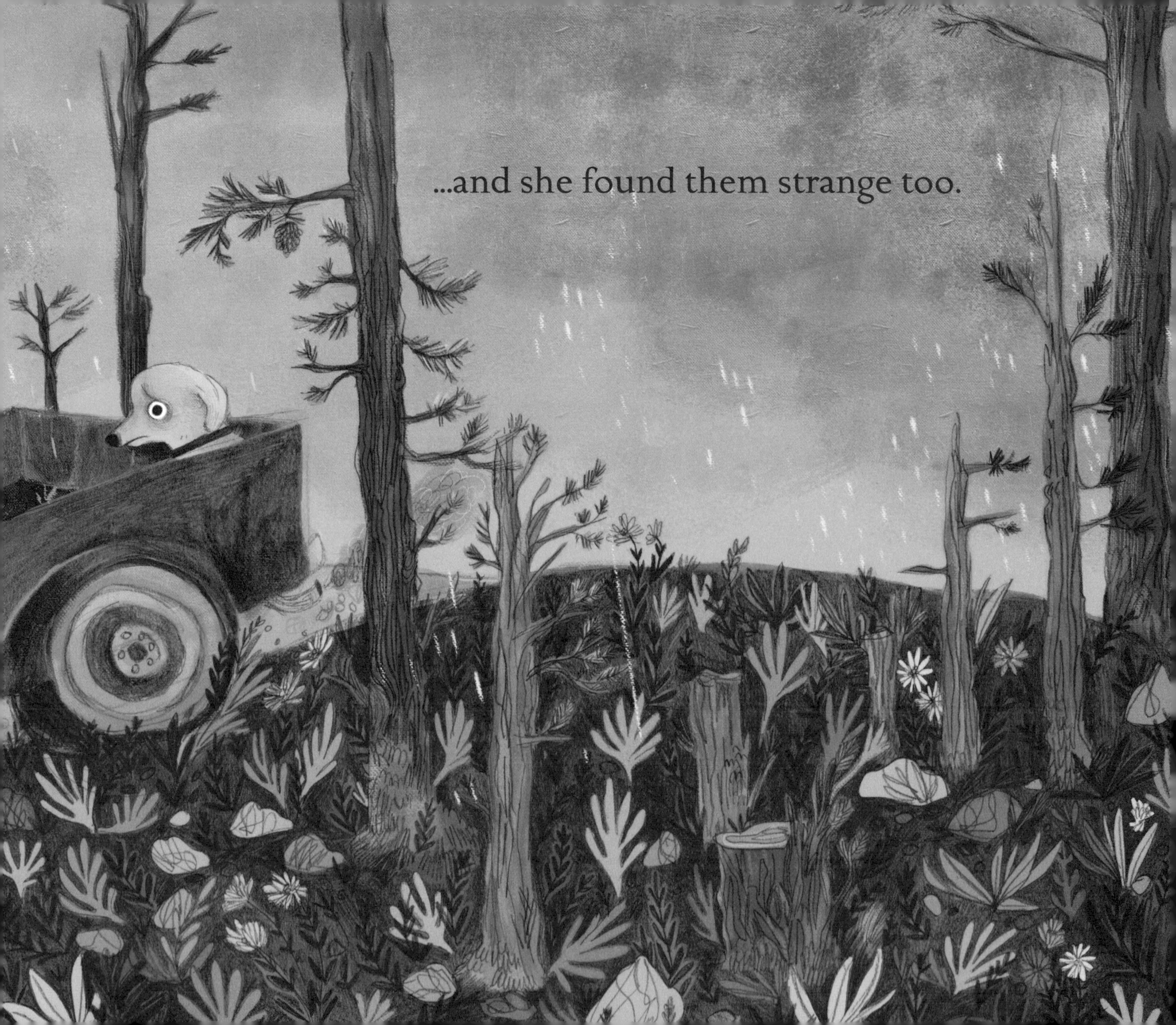

They did everything wrong!

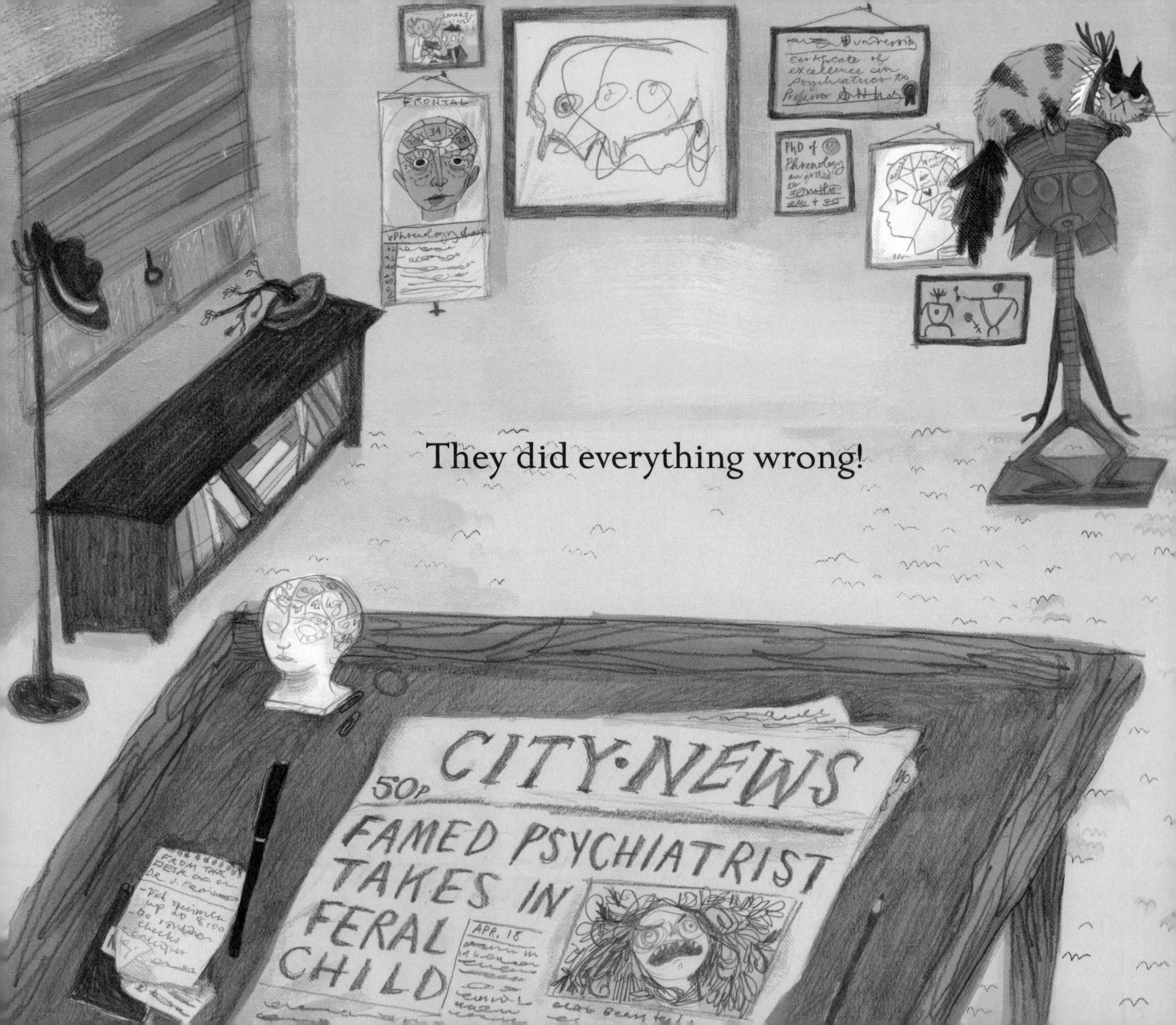

FRONTAL
Certificate of excellence in psychiatrics to
PhD of Phrenology awarded to
50p
CITY·NEWS
FAMED PSYCHIATRIST TAKES IN FERAL CHILD
FROM THE DESK OF

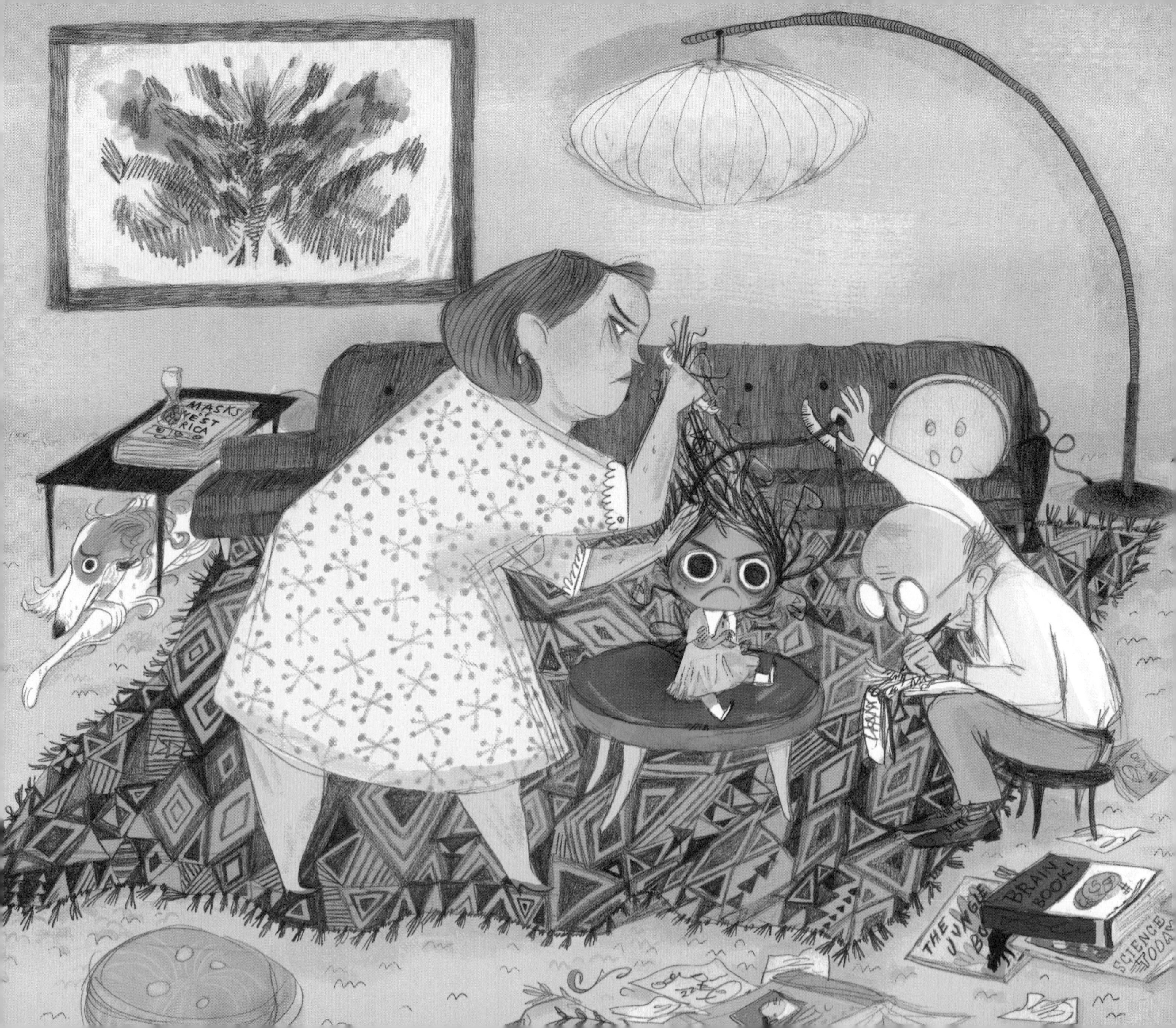
MASKS
BRAIN BOOK
THE JUNGLE
SCIENCE

They spoke wrong.

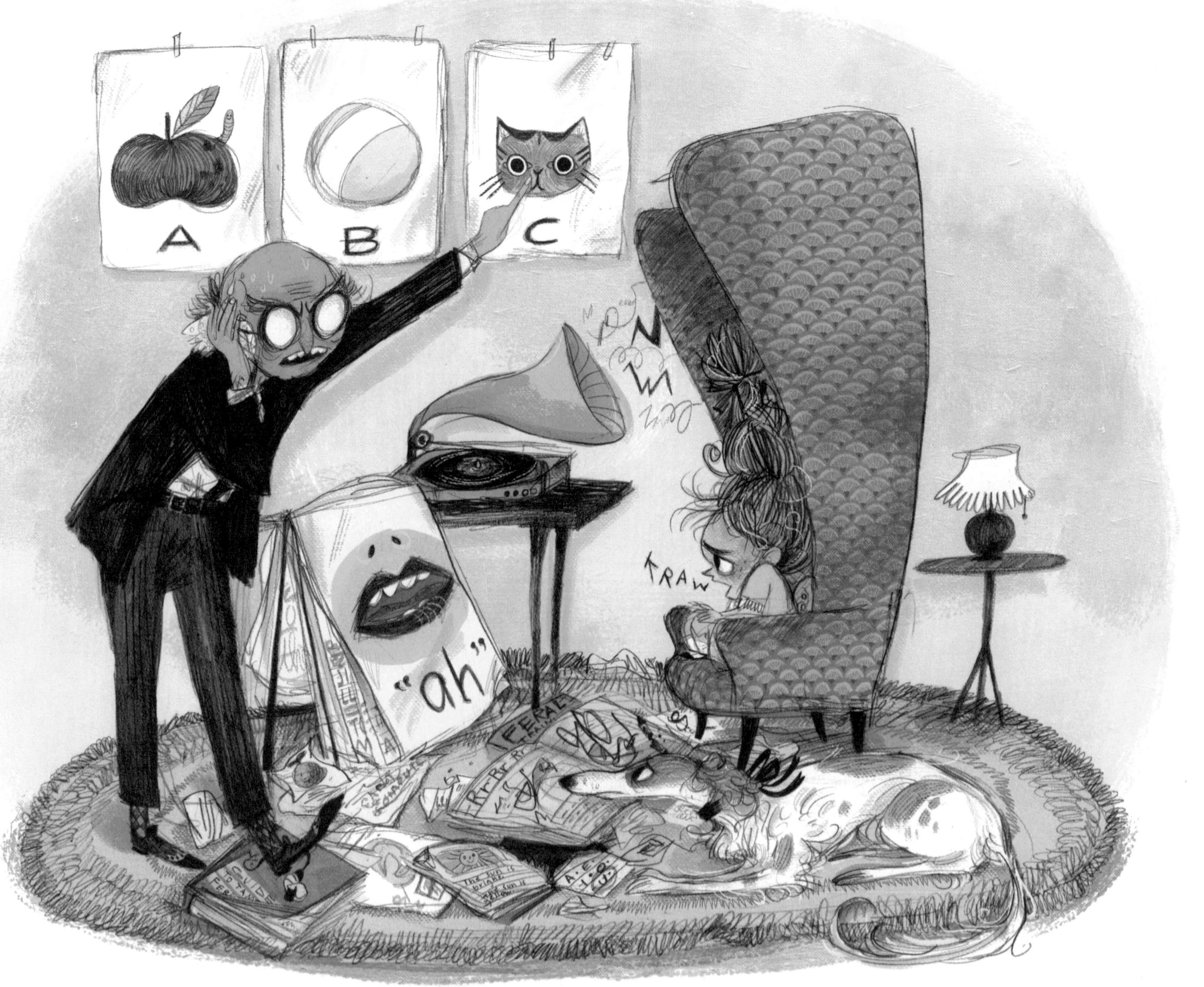
A
B
C
KRAW
"ah"
FERAL
Rr Rr Rr
The sun is bright
A E I O U

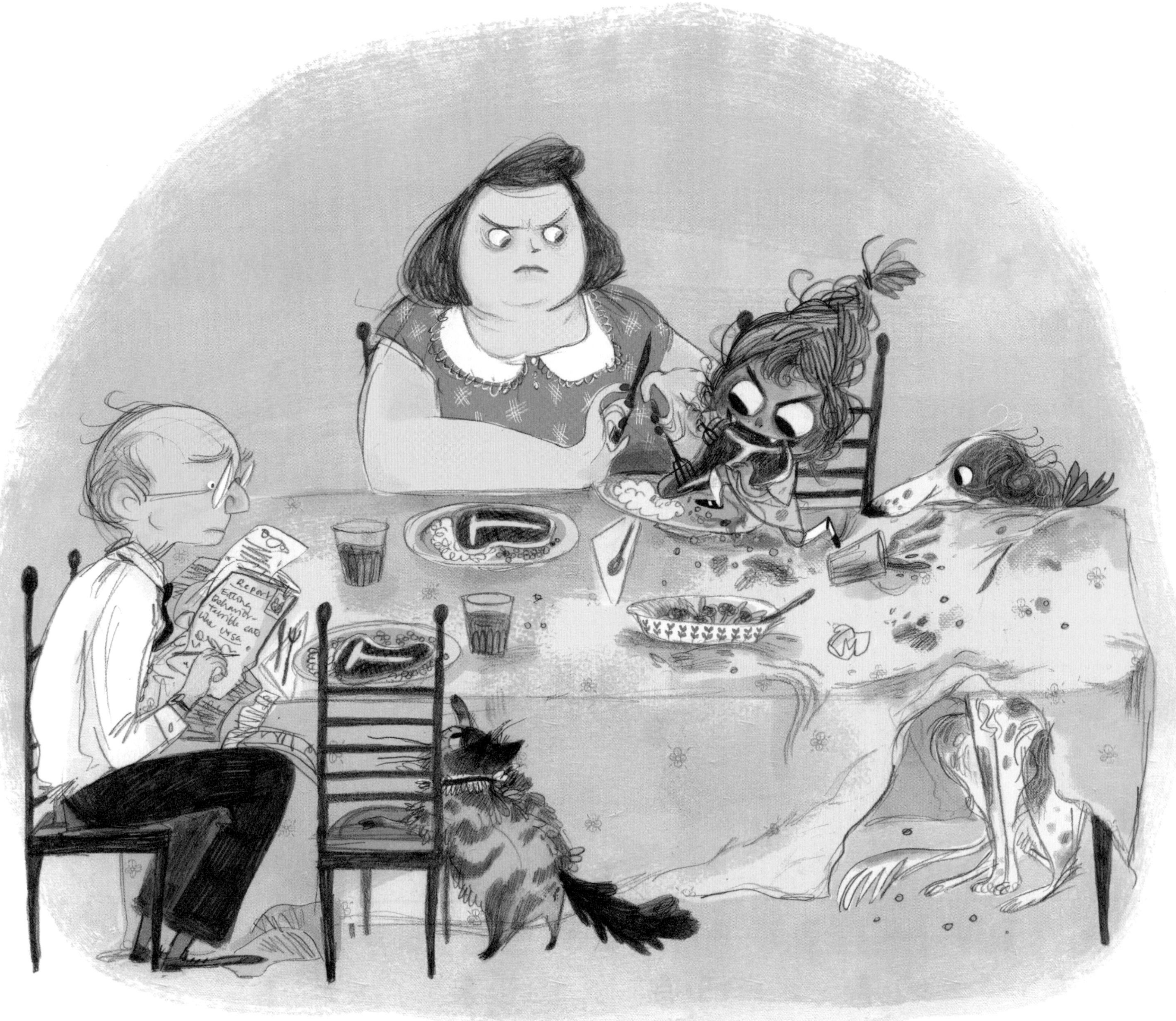
Report
Eating
Behavior-
Terrible eats

They ate wrong.

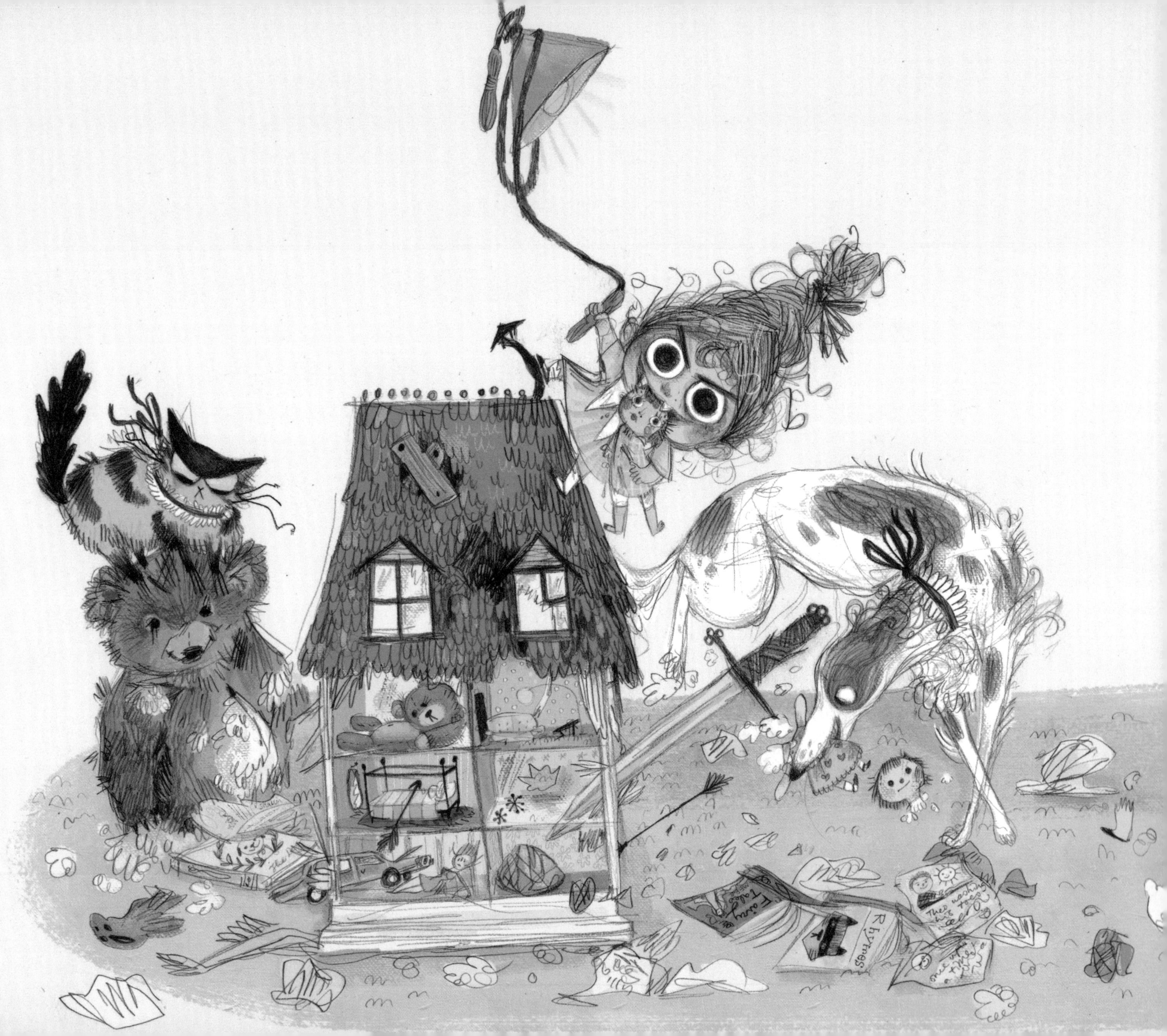

Fairy Tales
Rhymes

They played wrong.

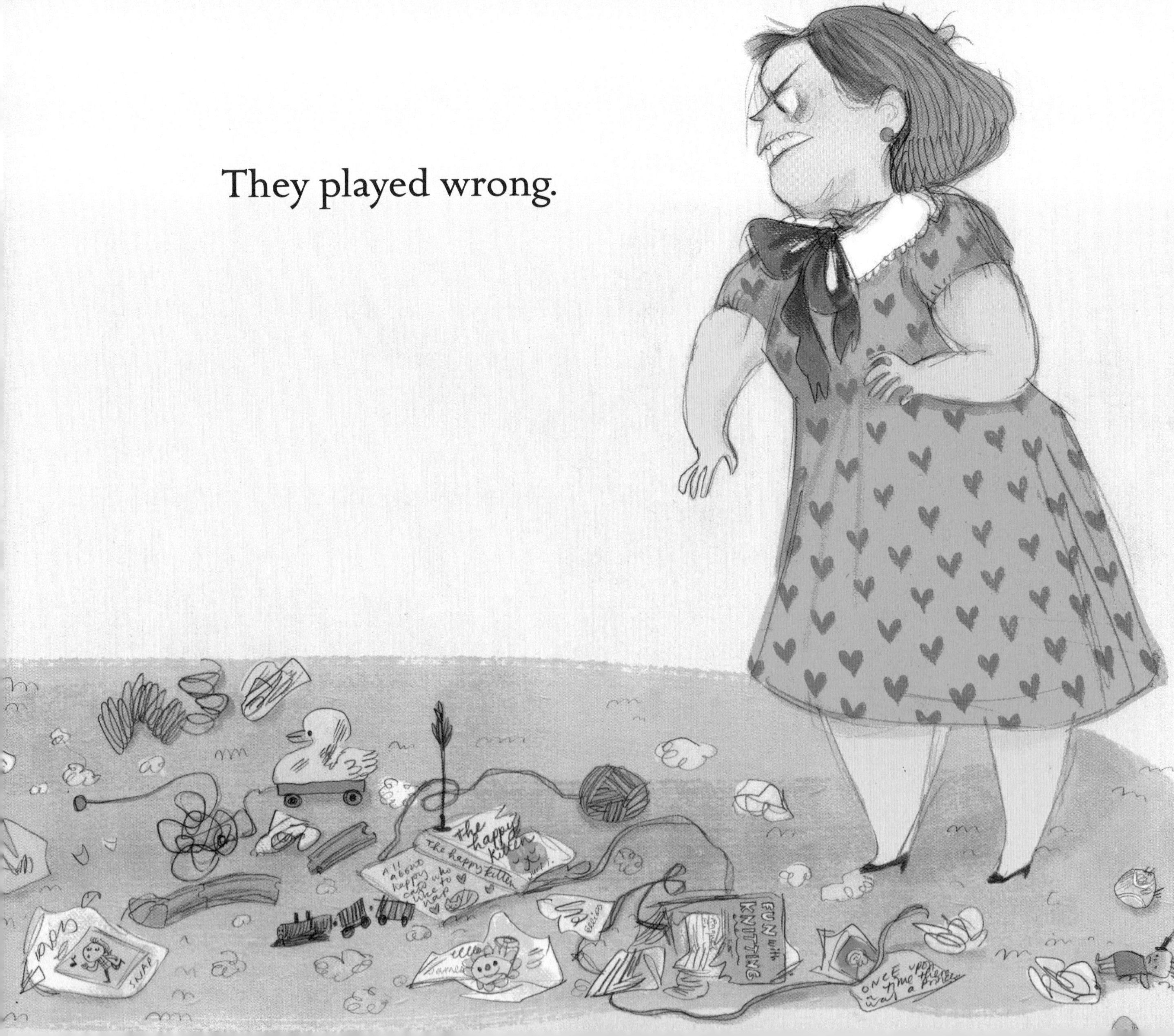

the happy kitten
The happy kitten
FUN with KNITTING

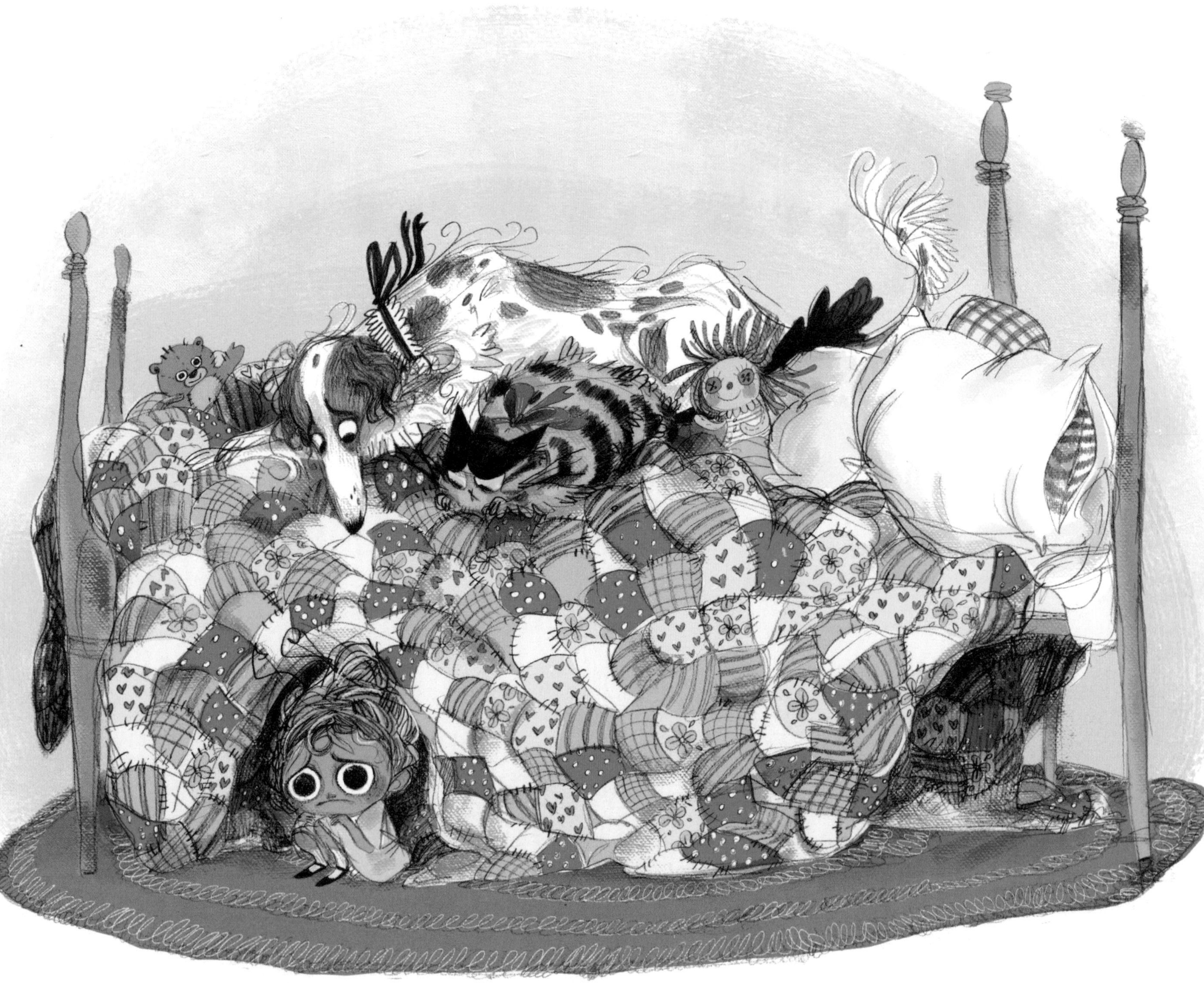

And she did not understand, and she was not happy.

Enough was enough!

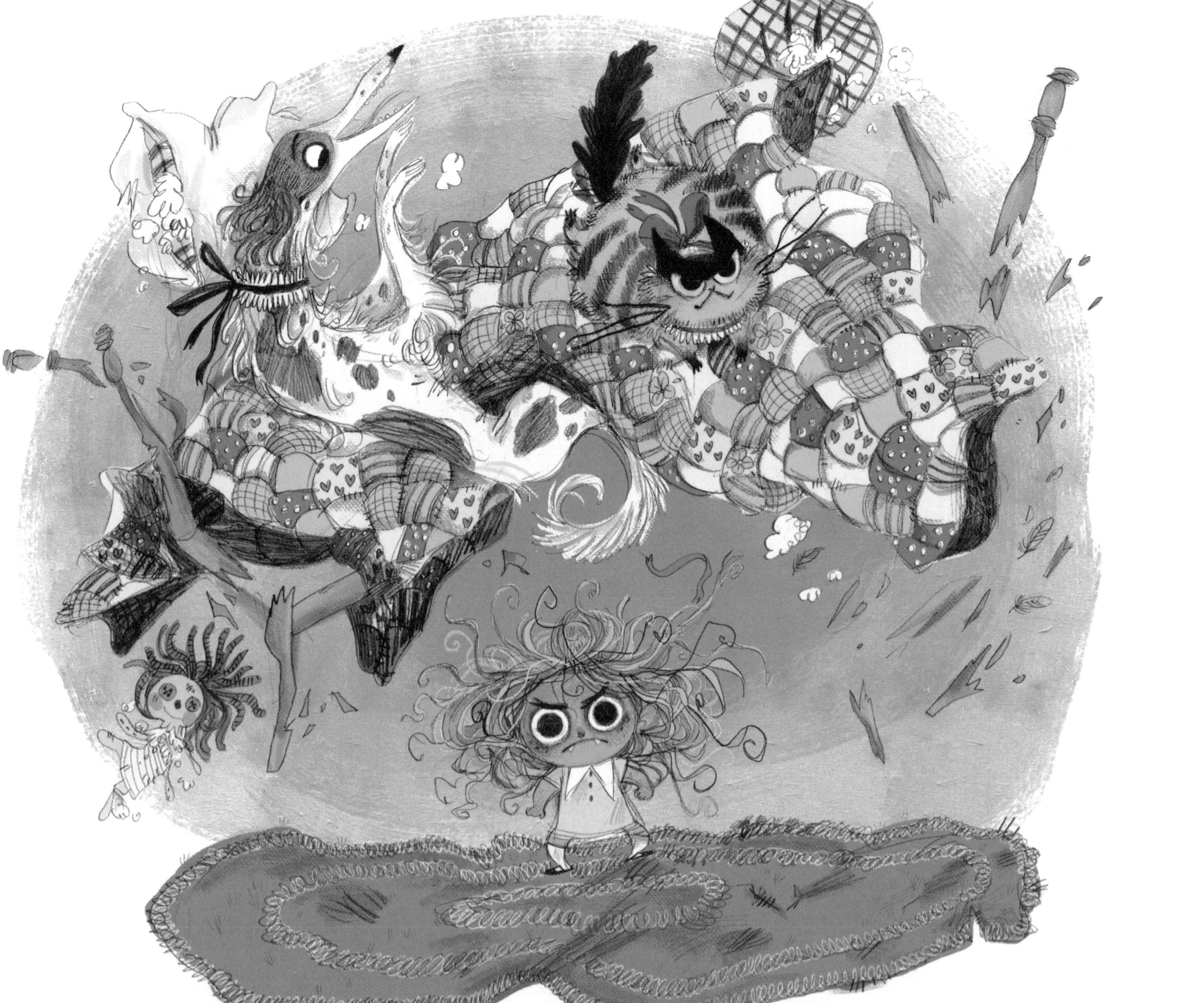

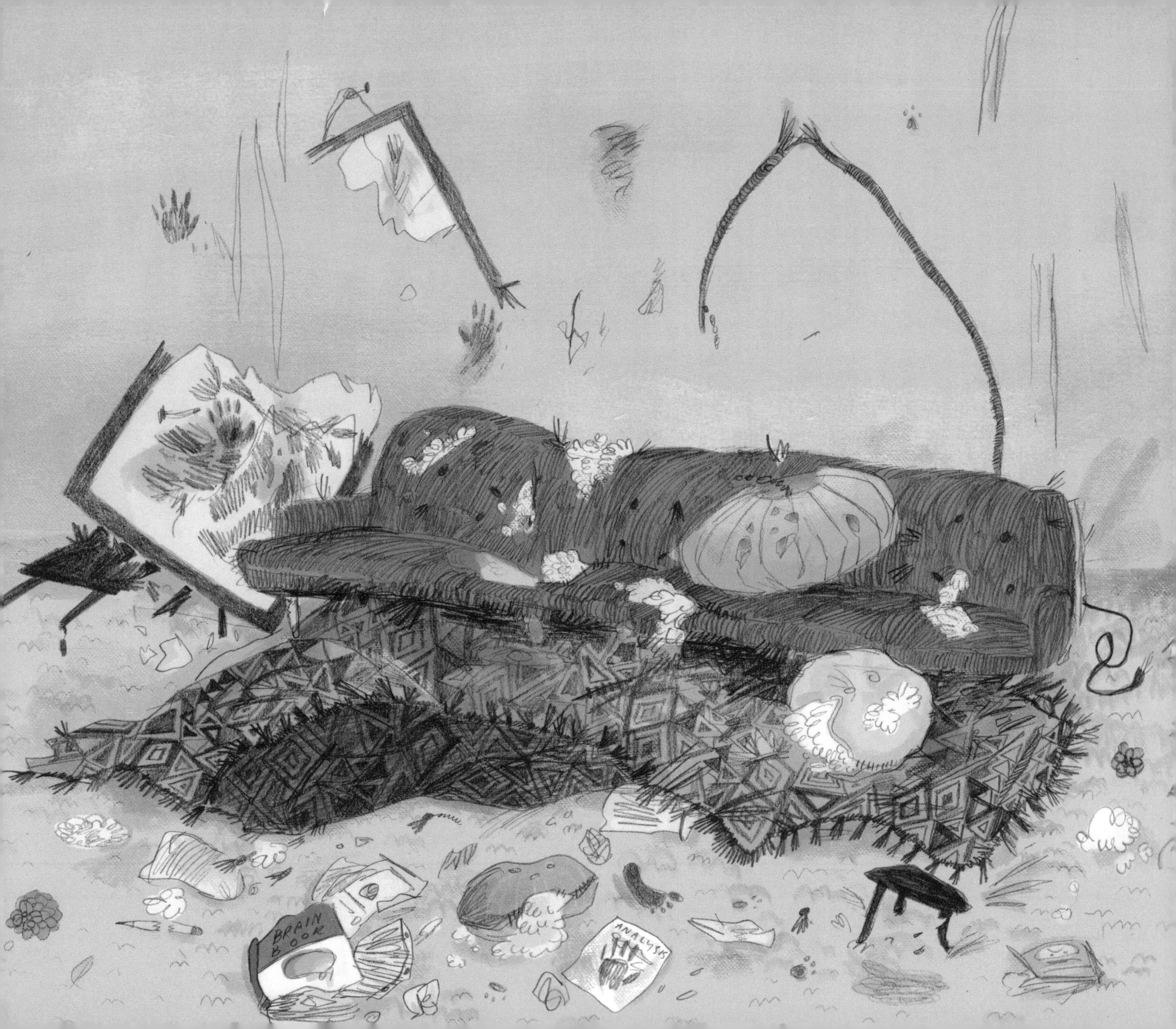
BRAIN BOOK
ANALYSIS

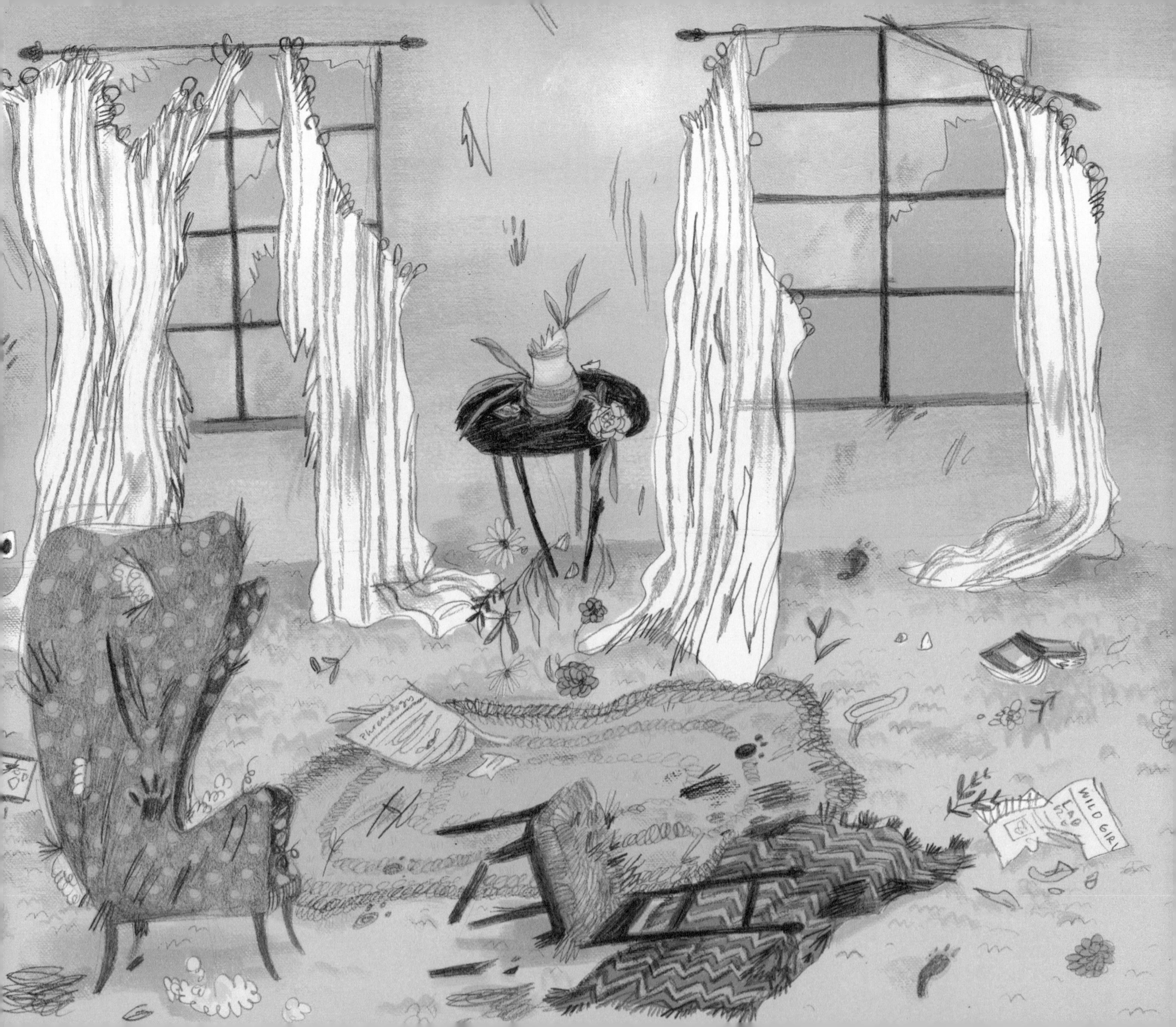
Phrenology
WILD GIRL

Everyone remembered how she left,
and all knew it was right.

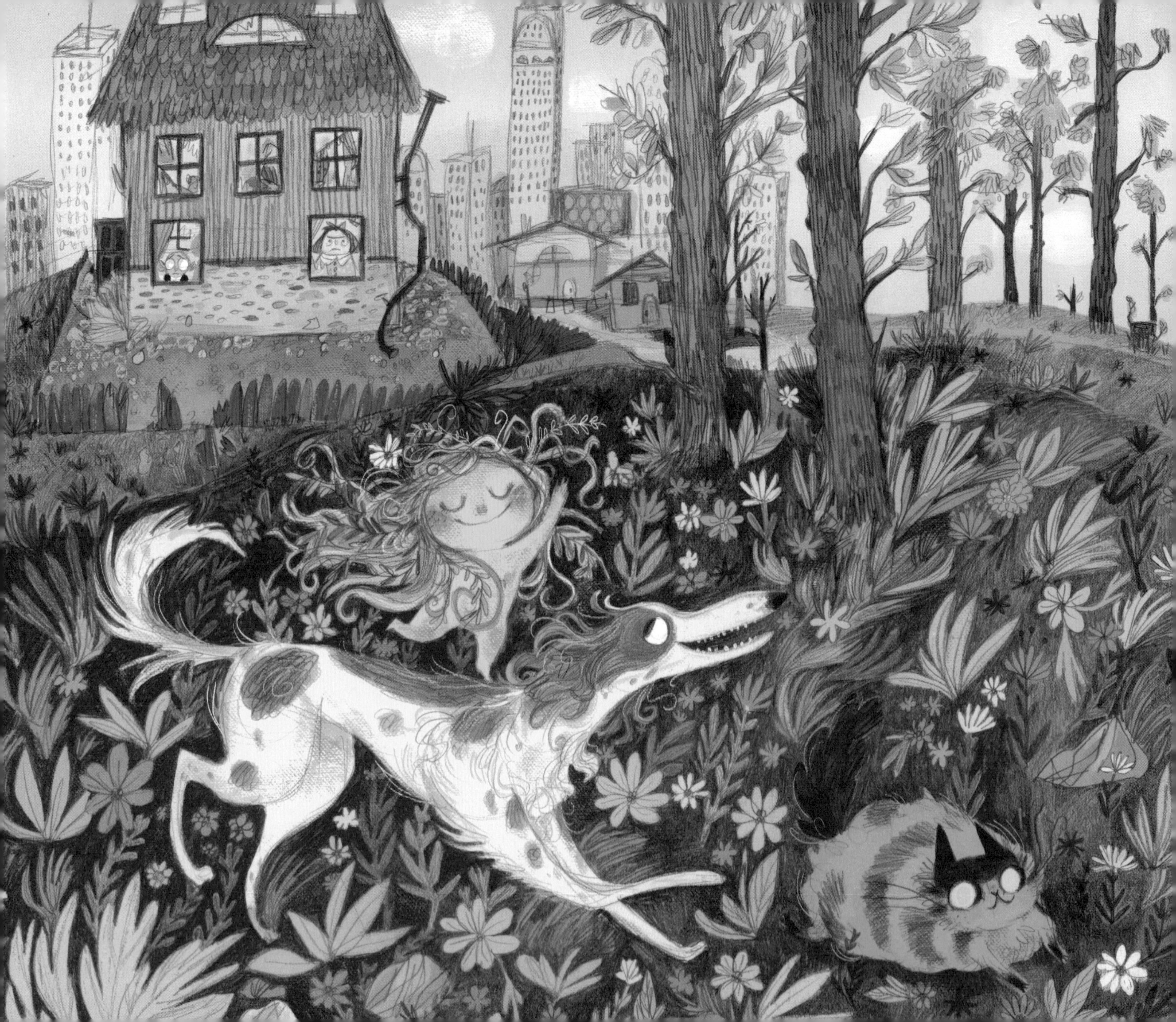

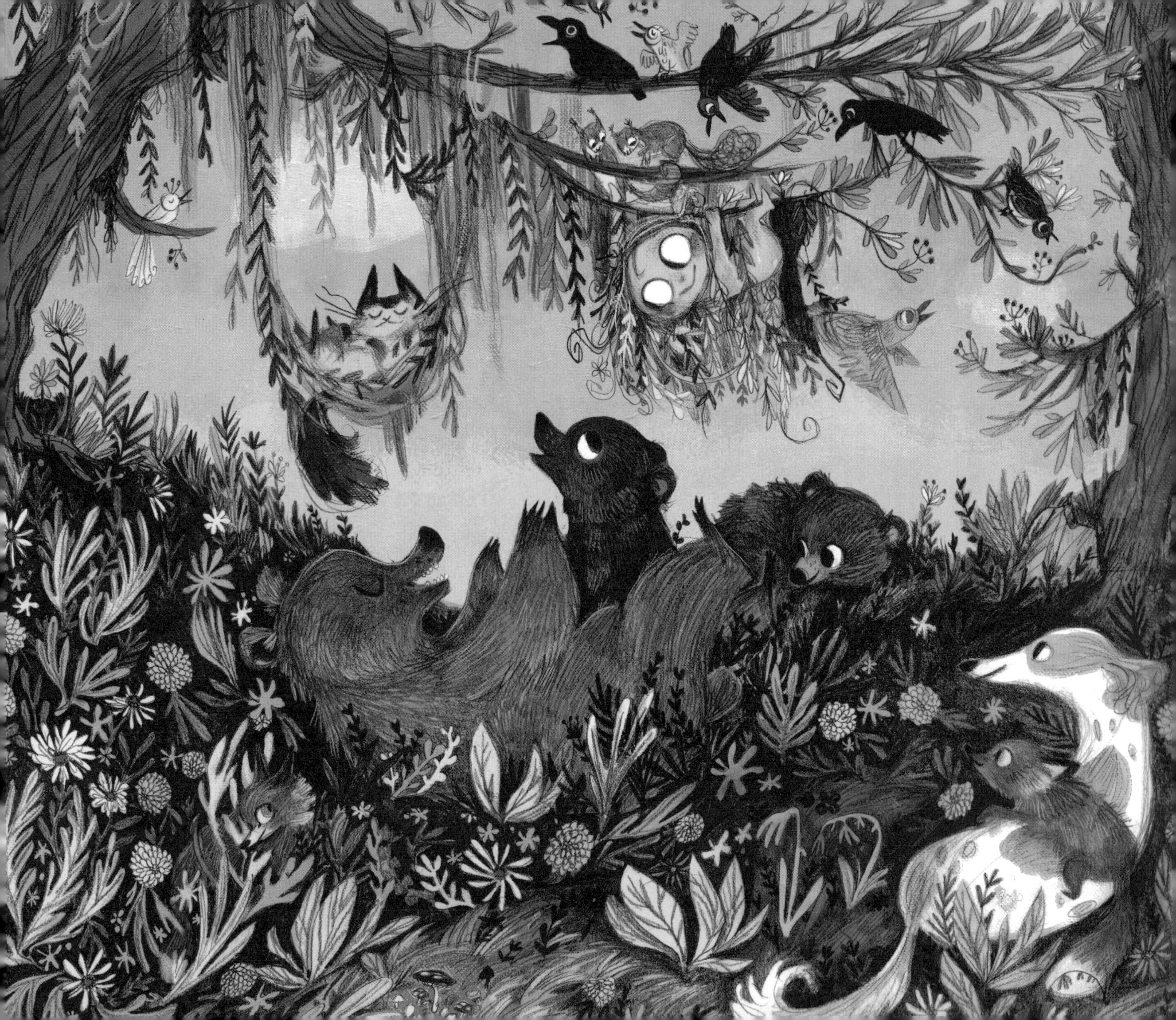

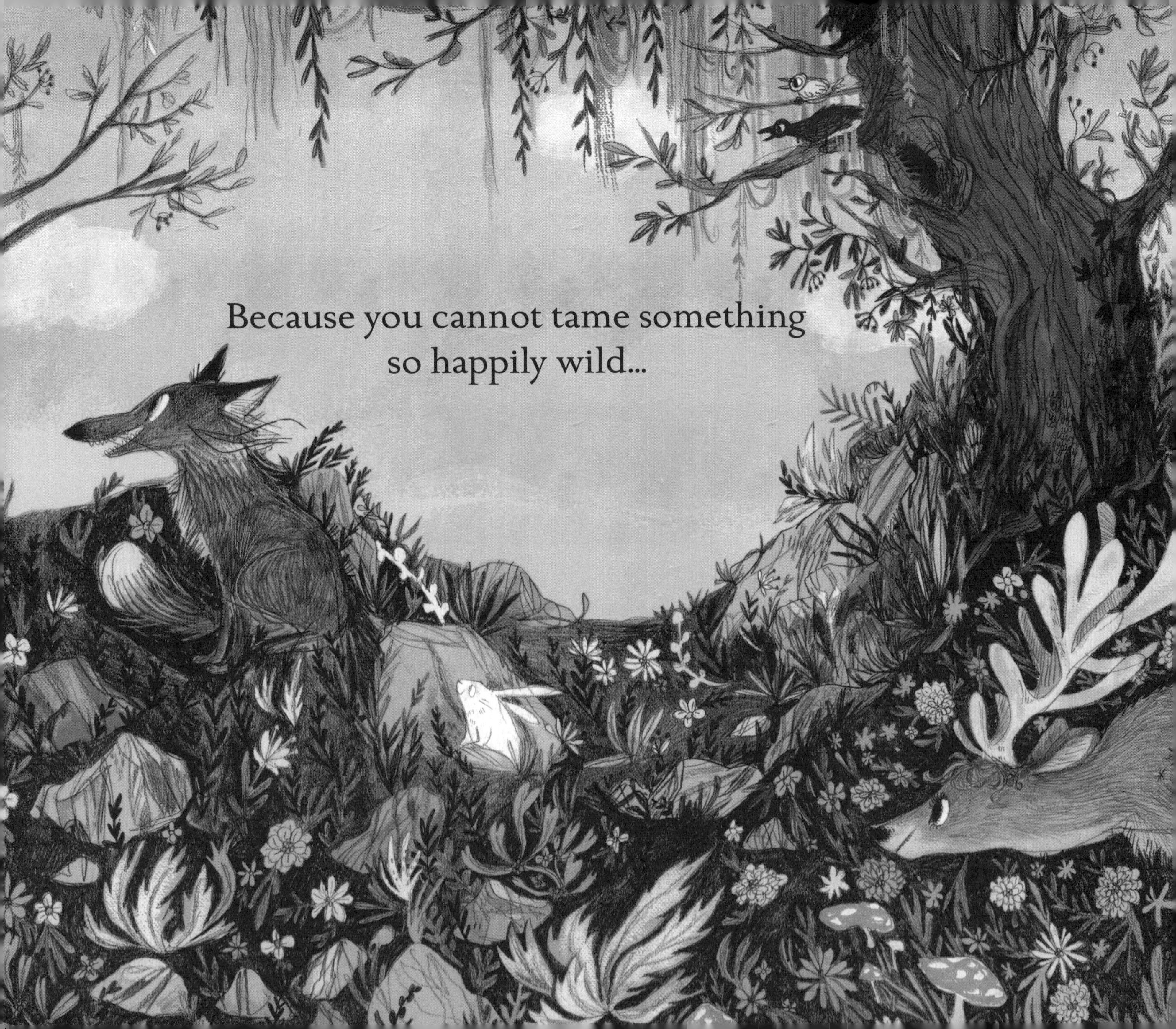

Because you cannot tame something
so happily wild...

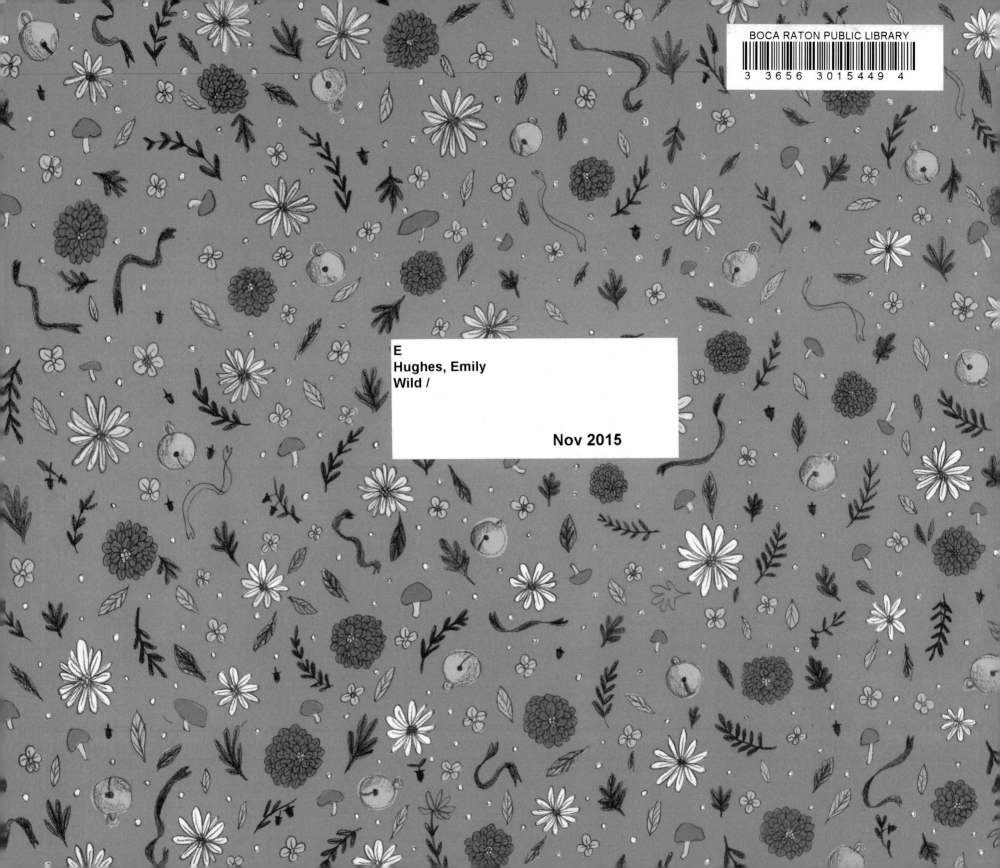